by Michael T. Riley

Grosset & Dunlap
An Imprint of Penguin Random House

GROSSET & DUNLAP
Penguin Young Readers Group
An Imprint of Penguin Random House LLC

The publisher does not have any control over and does not assume any responsibility for author or third-party websites or their content.

Additional illustrations by Dave Bardin.

Baseball field illustration: p. 45: Elinedesignservices/iStock/Thinkstock.

Major League Baseball trademarks and copyrights are used with permission of Major League Baseball Properties, Inc. Visit MLB.com. Used under license by Penguin Young Readers Group. All rights reserved. Published in 2017 by Grosset & Dunlap, an imprint of Penguin Random House LLC, 345 Hudson Street, New York, New York 10014. GROSSET & DUNLAP is a trademark of Penguin Random House LLC. Printed in the USA.

ISBN 9780451533951

10 9 8 7 6 5 4 3 2 1

This playbook belongs to

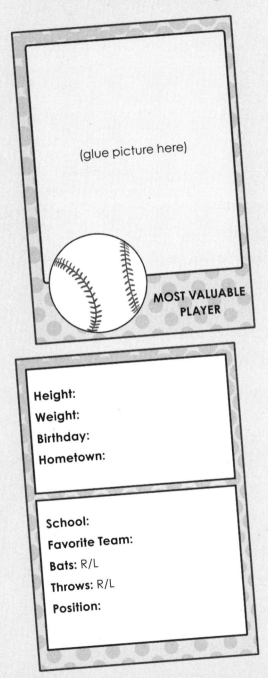

(glue picture here)

MOST VALUABLE PLAYER

Height:

Weight:

Birthday:

Hometown:

School:

Favorite Team:

Bats: R/L

Throws: R/L

Position:

Welcome to the Big Leagues! Break in your new playbook just like a baseball glove. Hold it in your glove hand and give the pocket a few thumps with your other hand, like an infielder preparing for the next hard grounder! Not too hard . . . there you go. Now you are ready for action!

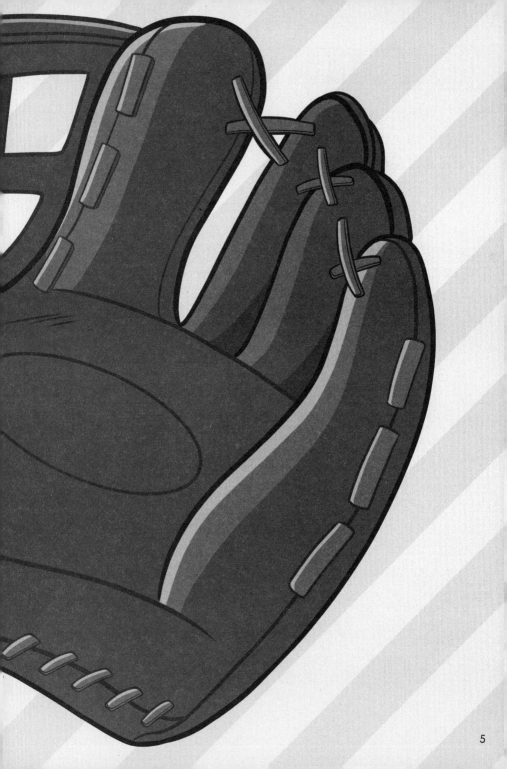

THINK FAST!

Major League hitters barely have time to think. A ninety-mile-per-hour fastball reaches home plate in .4167 seconds! Take a swing at these questions by trying to make your decisions as fast as the pros. Then quiz your friends!

- Who is your favorite baseball player? _____
- If you could be stranded on an island with one person, who would it be? _____
- If you could have the amazing skills of one professional athlete, who would it be and why? _____

  _____
- If you were an animal, what would you be? _____
- If you won a million dollars, what would you buy? _____
- If you could have one superpower, what would it be?

  _____
- If you could live anywhere in the world, where would it be?

  _____
- What was the most fun thing you did this week?

  _____
- What is the scariest thing you've ever seen?

  _____
- What word best describes you? _____

Are you smarter than the experts? Prove it by making your predictions for the upcoming *Major League Baseball* season. After the *World Series*, check back and see how you did!

Write your predictions here!

Division Champions:

American League East:

American League Central:

American League West:

National League East:

National League Central:

National League West:

Wild Card Winners:

***American League* Champions:**

***National League* Champions:**

***World Series* Champions:**

Tell your playbook about your likes and dislikes. Write your favorite things in fair territory, and discard everything else like a foul ball. Suggestions: type of music, movies, TV shows, celebrities, foods, school subjects, clothing styles, months, seasons, days of the week, sports, activities, animals, stores.

*Fact: Any ball that hits the foul pole is actually fair. Weird, right?

Fair

Foul

_____

_____

_____

_____

_____

_____

_____

_____

_____

_____

_____

STRIKE ZONE!

Every hitter is different. Some like a low, outside pitch. Others drool for that high cheddar! Using red and blue crayons or markers, color in the strike zone to show your hot and cold spots.

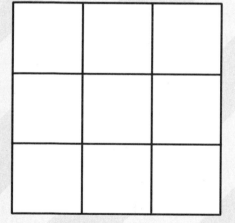

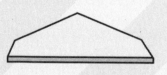

Now, write about a recent at-bat!

The batter has just blasted a pitch to deep left field. The outfielder has it in his sights. He's at the track, at the wall, looking up. He leaps and . . . Answer these questions to decode the message and find out what happens.

1. What is the home field of the *Chicago Cubs*?

   _ _ _ _ _(_)_ _ _ _ _ _

2. Which *Washington Nationals* outfielder debuted in the Majors at age nineteen? _ _ _ _ _

   _(_)_ _ _ _

3. What is the nickname of *Mariners* pitcher Felix Hernandez? _(_)_ _

4. What color is the *Phillie Phanatic*? _(_)_ _ _

5. Who is the star catcher for the *San Francisco Giants*?

   _ _ _ _ _ _ _(_)_ _ _

6. What is the *Milwaukee Brewers* mascot's tradition after a home run? (_)_ _ _ _

7. What team has Joe Mauer played with for more than twelve years? (_)_ _ _ _

8. Which is the only *MLB* team with a home outside the United States? _ _(_)_ _ _ _ _

9. The Cy Young Award is won by the best player at what position? _ _(_)_ _ _ _

10. What type of slow-traveling pitch looks like a fastball at first? _ ⃝_ _ _ _ _ _

11. What spot in the batting order do pitchers usually hit? _ _ _⃝_

12. What is the highest section of seats in a stadium often called? _ _ _⃝_ _ _ _ _

(The circled letter in each answer corresponds with its question number in the decoded message.)

Decoded message:

_ _'_ _ _ _ _ _ _ _ _ _!
3 9'6 5 8 11 7 2 10 1 4 12!

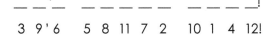

13

AUTOGRAPH PAD

You never know when you'll get to meet your favorite ballplayers. Collect autographs here for safekeeping!

Player: _____

Date: _____

Place: _____

Player: _____

Date: _____

Place: _____

Player: _____

Date: _____

Place: _____

Player: _____

Date: _____

Place: _____

Player: _____

Date: _____

Place: _____

Player: _____

Date: _____

Place: _____

Player: _____

Date: _____

Place: _____

Player: _____

Date: _____

Place: _____

Every *Major League* ballpark has its quirks. *Fenway Park* in Boston has a massive left-field wall called the *Green Monster*. *Kauffman Stadium* boasts more than three hundred feet of fountains. And *Diamondbacks* fans cool off in an outfield swimming pool at *Chase Field*! Write about your home. In what ways is it unique? What are your favorite things to do around the house?

_____

_____

_____

_____

_____

_____

_____

_____

_____

_____

_____

_____

BUILD YOUR OWN BALLPARK!

Sketch the design for your favorite team's new state-of-the-art ballpark. Be sure to give it a cool name, and label all the zany and unusual attractions you've invented to thrill your hometown fans!

ROAD TRIP!

MLB players play eighty-one games each year away from home. That's a lot of time on the road! Have you ever gone on a really awesome trip? Tell the story about where you went and all the cool things that happened.

_____

_____

_____

_____

_____

_____

_____

_____

_____

_____

_____

_____

_____

JERSEY JUMBLE

Something has gone haywire with the names on these jerseys! Unscramble the letters to get these star players' uniforms ready for game time, and write each name in the space below.

HYEDRAW
22

1. H _ Y W _ _ D

HOCO
17

2. C _ _ _

KATASUMSO
8

3. M _ _ S _ _ K _ _

WHIGWARNIT
50

4. W _ _ N _ _ _ G _ _

5. _ _ B _ _ R _

6. T _ _ O _ I _ _ K _

7. M _ _ U _ C _ E _

8. _ A _ H _ _ O

9. _ T _ N _ _ N

10. G _ _ D _ C _ _ I _ _

25

Spring Training is when teams get in tip-top shape. For six weeks, do something active every day, even if it's only a few jumping jacks! Then keep a log of what you did.

Week 1

_____

_____

_____

_____

_____

_____

Week 2

_____

_____

_____

_____

_____

_____

Week 3

_____

_____

_____

_____

_____

_____

_____

Week 4

_____

_____

_____

_____

_____

_____

_____

Week 5

_____

_____

_____

_____

_____

_____

_____

Week 6

_____

_____

_____

_____

_____

_____

_____

What were your favorite things that you did during your six weeks of training? What did you learn? Write about it here!

_____

_____

_____

_____

_____

_____

_____

_____

_____

_____

_____

_____

_____

_____

_____

_____

From slugger Edwin Encarnacion "walking the parrot" to Jose Bautista's famous bat flip, players have invented many creative home run celebrations. Think about going yard in the *Major Leagues*. How would you celebrate? Be unique!

_____

_____

_____

_____

_____

_____

_____

_____

_____

_____

_____

_____

_____

_____

_____

Across

3. High-pressure role for Kimbrel, Davis

5. Long-time *Yankees* first baseman Mark _____

9. Dee Gordon loves getting the _____ sign

10. Warming up in the _____

Down

1. Watery landing for *Giants* splash hits: McCovey _____

2. Excited *Braves* fans do the _____

4. 2015 *World Series Champions*, the _____

6. The batter is out on an _____ fly

7. A _____ delay makes fans run for cover

8. A _____ play is a pitcher's best friend

33

Major League pitchers throw many different pitches, from Noah Syndergaard's blazing fastball to R.A. Dickey's dancing knuckleball. Imagine you are on the mound. Invent your own pitch!

What is it called?

_____

_____

_____

_____

_____

_____

How do you grip the baseball?

_____

_____

_____

_____

_____

_____

_____

What type of throwing motion do you use?

_____

_____

_____

_____

_____

How fast does it travel?

_____

_____

_____

_____

_____

Does it do anything wonky to fool the batter?

_____

_____

_____

_____

_____

Friends often disagree when picking their favorite *Major League* teams. Some good-natured bickering over baseball is part of being a fan. List your friends and their loyalties. That way you'll know who to brag to when your team makes the *World Series*!

Name: _____

Favorite team: _____

Name: _____

Favorite team: _____

Name: _____

Favorite team: _____

Name: _____

Favorite team: _____

Name: _____

Favorite team: _____

Name: _____

Favorite team: _____

It's Game 7 of the *World Series* and you are the manager! Fill in the card below to create the ultimate lineup. Use current players, former players, or even your friends!

No.	Player	Position
1		
2		
3		
4		
5		
6		
7		
8		
9		

Substitutes

Bullpen

WORD SEARCH

Can you find and circle the names and terms below? They may appear across, up and down, or diagonally.

Slider

Playoffs

Athletics

Center Field

Grand Slam

Bunt

Astros

Lineup

Rookie

Mike Trout

Doubleheader

```
S F W A C O S Z E G D H N X D A
X F B P F E G N R O L O Y V I T
W B F E U S N A I G N A F O V H
R U T O M Q N T D I J B X E L L
E N K I Y D S T E L I N E U P E
D T X W S A T U O R T E K I M T
I E H L W Q L F R S F M W D Y I
L U A B U V B P U X R I H F S C
S M T Z Y L N O X X N T E O Z S
R D O U B L E H E A D E R L V P
H O E Z Y A A U X D Y T N I D M
L T O W I U H U D Q S A Y U M H
X X N K J K N R F A C Y A N N Z
G Y F H I O Q G W U B Y G Q X S
J G K K C E E W Q T G K O F E B
W W U W W A D N A Q M C O E P D
```

Every fan remembers seeing a live *Major League* game for the first time. Write about your first trip to the ballpark.

I went to the game with . . .

_____

_____

_____

When I saw the size of the field, I thought . . .

_____

_____

_____

In person, the players looked . . .

_____

_____

_____

The final score was . . .

_____

_____

_____

The most spectacular plays were . . .

_____

_____

_____

The best thing I ate at the ballpark was . . .

_____

_____

_____

Some other great memories were . . .

_____

_____

_____

Major League players choose the music that plays just before their at-bats. Yoenis Cespedes actually let a local singer and Mets fan compose a new song called "The Power" just for him! Unleash your musical side and write the lyrics to your own entrance tune.

What is this all about? Fill in the bubbles so fans can see what these two are saying to each other.

45

MY FIRST CONTRACT!

Negotiate like the pros! Take this contract to the general manager (your parents), agree to terms, and sign on the dotted lines!

Baseball Season Contract

Date: _____

I, _____, "*Future All-Star*," hereby agree to
    (YOUR NAME HERE)
perform all the duties listed below, assigned and agreed upon by

_____.
    (PARENT/GUARDIAN)

Starting on Opening Day and through the end of the *World Series*, I will:

1. _____

2. _____

3. _____

4. _____

5. _____

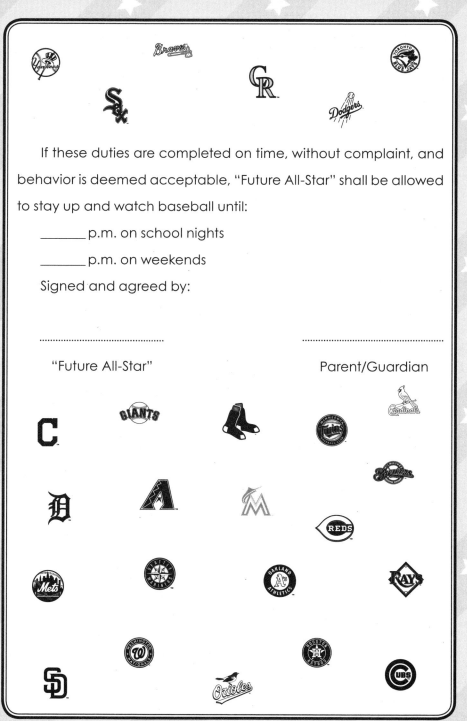

If these duties are completed on time, without complaint, and behavior is deemed acceptable, "Future All-Star" shall be allowed to stay up and watch baseball until:

_____ p.m. on school nights

_____ p.m. on weekends

Signed and agreed by:

....

"Future All-Star"   Parent/Guardian

IN A PICKLE!

In your fridge, a pickle is a cucumber preserved in brine. In baseball, it's when a base runner is in big trouble because he is caught between the bases. Have you ever been "in a pickle" at home or in school? Write about it (we won't tell!).

_____

_____

_____

_____

_____

_____

_____

_____

_____

_____

_____

_____

_____

_____

LAUNDRY MISHAP!

These star players are ready for action, but their numbers have fallen off in the wash! Draw them back on so they can take the field. Then draw in the rest of the players' bodies (don't forget their heads, too!).

1. SYNDERGAARD

2. SEAGER

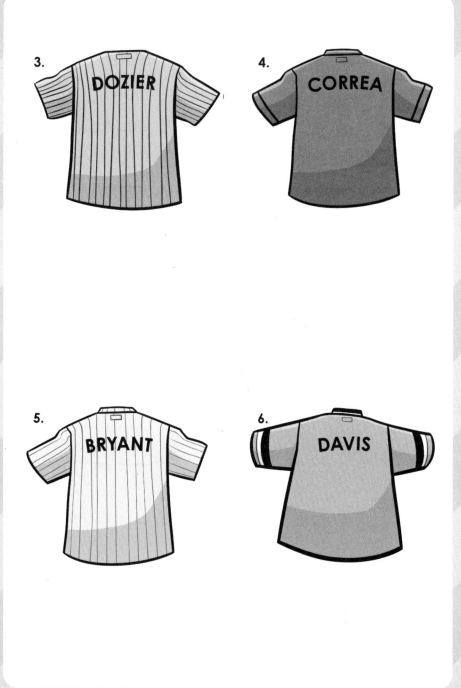

3. DOZIER

4. CORREA

5. BRYANT

6. DAVIS

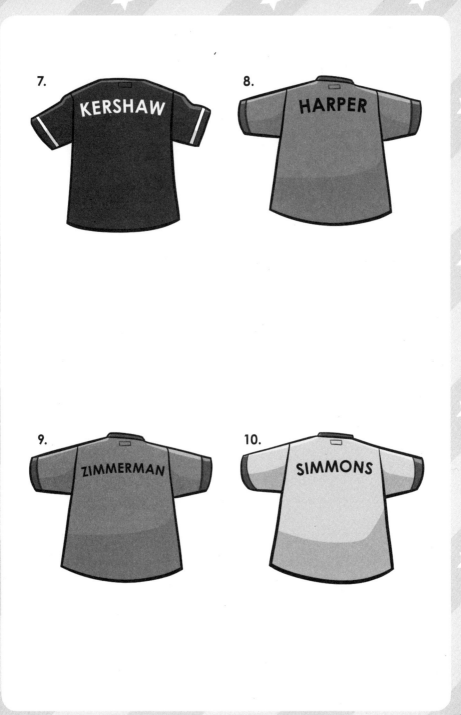

7.

KERSHAW

8.

HARPER

9.

ZIMMERMAN

10.

SIMMONS

WORD CHALLENGE

Catcher Jarrod Saltalamacchia has the longest last name in baseball history! How many words can you make using only the letters found in SALTALAMACCHIA? List them below!

_____   _____

_____   _____

_____   _____

_____   _____

_____   _____

_____   _____

_____   _____

_____   _____

_____   _____

_____   _____

_____   _____

_____   _____

_____   _____

_____   _____

_____   _____

_____   _____

_____   _____

_____   _____

_____   _____

_____   _____

How many did you find?

25 words = Top prospect!

50 words = All-Star!

100 words or more = Hall of Famer!

"I GOT IT!"

This fielder is trying to catch a pop-up in the swirling Chicago winds. Find the right path from the air to his glove by tracing the correct line.

You are a local newspaper reporter assigned to interview your favorite player for a column about tonight's game. Think of some questions, imagine his responses (or role-play with a friend), and then get that column done before the deadline! Include a headline, photo, and caption.

Headline: _____

Photo

Photo Caption: _____

_____   _____

_____   _____

_____   _____

_____

The "interlocking NY," which represents the *Yankees*, is one of the most celebrated logos in *Major League Baseball*. Fill in the missing lines to complete the design (then, if you're a *Red Sox* fan, draw a red circle around it and cross over it!).

TM

Use this space to draw your favorite team logos, or invent your own!

Which nickname belongs to each ballplayer? Draw lines to match them up!

1. Albert Pujols
2. Matt Harvey
3. Jose Altuve
4. Pedro Alvarez
5. Aroldis Chapman
6. David Wright
7. Pablo Sandoval
8. Mike Trout
9. Yasiel Puig
10. Chris Sale

a. Captain America
b. Wild Horse
c. The Condor
d. Dark Knight
e. Gigante
f. The Machine
g. Cuban Missile
h. Kung Fu Panda
i. Millville Meteor
j. El Toro

Think of some cool baseball nicknames for you and your friends!

Friend: _____

Nickname: _____

Reason: _____

Friend: _____

Nickname: _____

Reason: _____

Friend: _____

Nickname: _____

Reason: _____

Friend: _____

Nickname: _____

Reason: _____

Friend: _____

Nickname: _____

Reason: _____

Your nickname: _____

Reason: _____

Even Big Leaguers make embarrassing mistakes from time to time, like dropping a pop fly or forgetting how many outs have been made in the inning. What was your most embarrassing moment?

_____

_____

_____

_____

_____

_____

_____

_____

_____

_____

_____

_____

_____

_____

Every great play in baseball leaves a mark. Next time you get dirty for the team, wipe some infield clay or grass onto this page as a memento. Then tell the story of the diving catch or fearless slide that helped your team win the game.

Baseball players and coaches secretly strategize using signs. With your friends, invent your own language of signals. Tug your ear, wiggle your fingers, or do anything you can imagine. Sketch each sign and what it means, and keep these pages a secret!

Sign   ## Meaning

_____

_____

_____

_____

_____

_____

_____

_____

_____

_____

Meaning

_____
_____
_____
_____
_____

Sign

Sign

Meaning

_____
_____
_____
_____
_____

Sign

Meaning

_____

_____

_____

_____

_____

_____

_____

_____

Meaning

Sign

_____

_____

_____

_____

_____

_____

_____

_____

Sign

Meaning

_____
_____
_____
_____
_____
_____

Meaning

Sign

_____
_____
_____
_____
_____
_____

You have just stepped into the batter's box for your first *Major League* at-bat. Describe this monumental experience—the sights, the sounds, even the smells. How do you feel?

_____

_____

_____

_____

_____

_____

_____

_____

_____

_____

_____

_____

_____

_____

_____

_____

Now, draw yourself on TV!

SEVENTH INNING STRETCH!

During a baseball game, the time between the top and bottom of the seventh inning is when fans get up and stretch. In this book, it is time to get some fresh air! That's right, put this book down right now and go outside! Run around! Play catch! Pretend you are Bryce Harper and blast a pitch into the neighbor's yard! Then come back and write about the fun you just had.

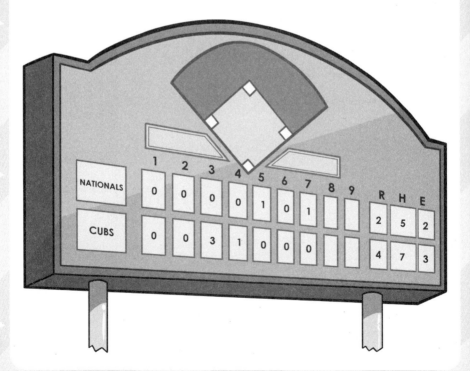

IT'S COMIC TIME!

Write a comic starring your favorite team playing its fiercest rival in a showdown for the ages!

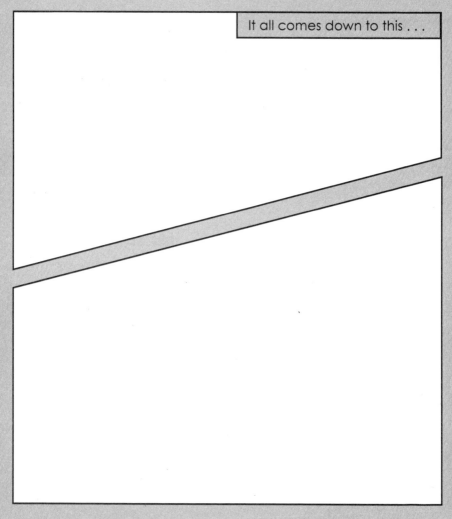

It all comes down to this . . .

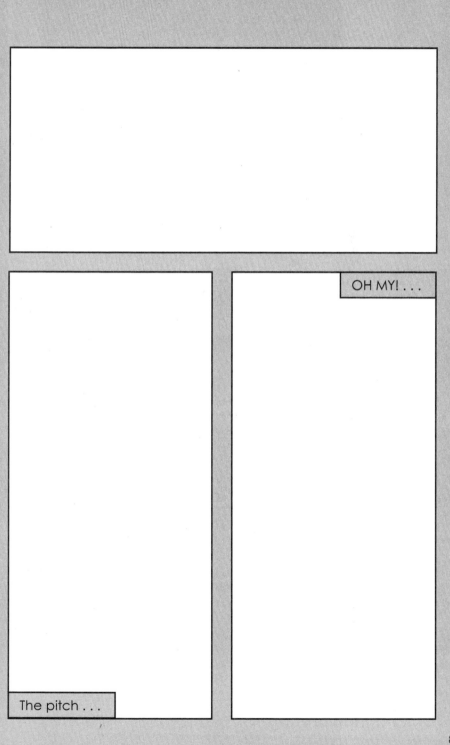

The pitch . . .

OH MY! . . .

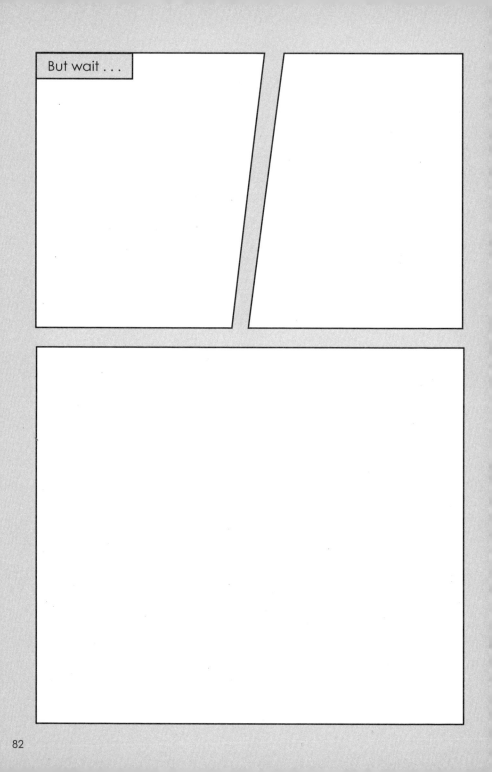

But wait . . .

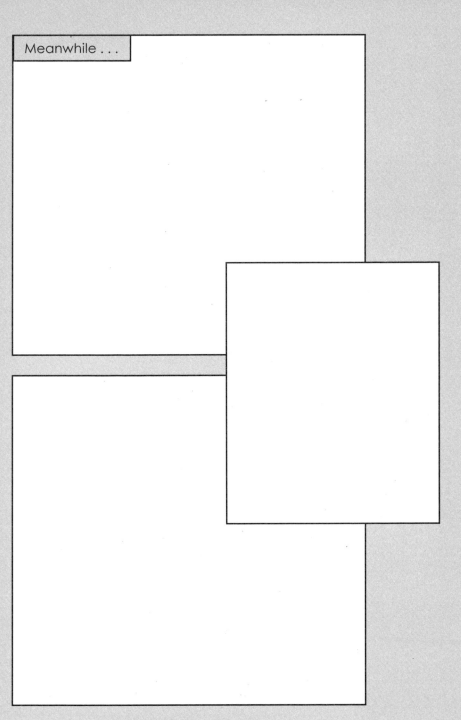

Meanwhile . . .

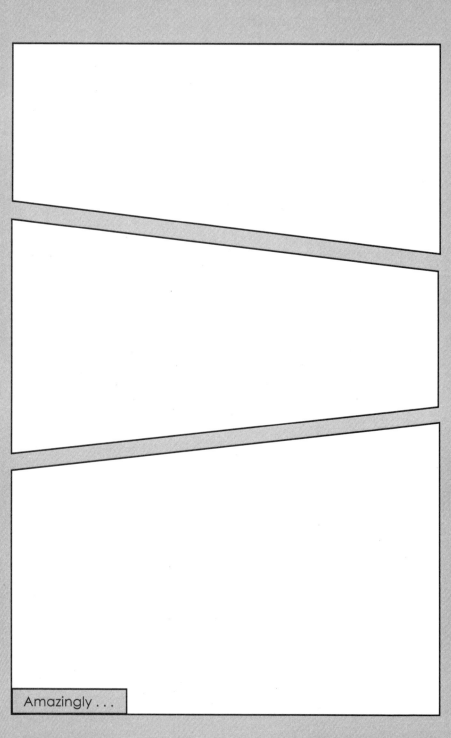

Amazingly . . .

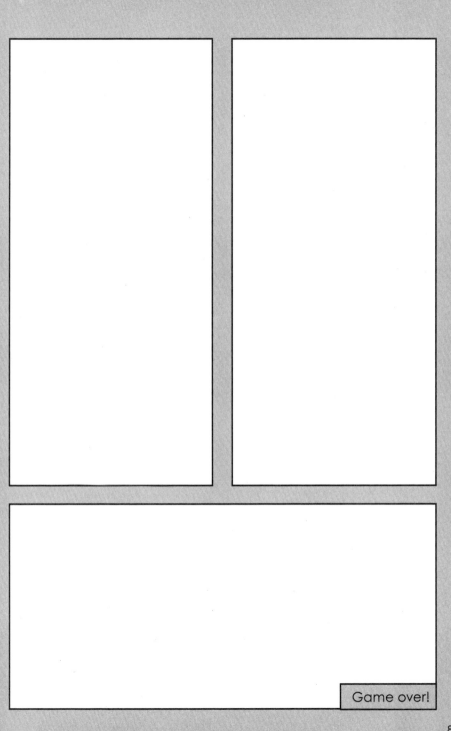

Game over!

PLAYOFF BEARDS!

Some superstitious players believe that beards can bring good luck in the *Postseason*. Help these clean-shaven players reach the *World Series* by giving them some October scruff!

What is one strange routine that you use to drum up good luck? Write about it in the space on the next page.

FIRST PITCH FRIGHT

You are about to throw out the ceremonial first pitch at a *Major League Baseball* game when you become so nervous, you see four catchers! Take a deep breath. Then find the real catcher by spotting the one that is slightly different from the rest.

GLOBAL MATCHING GAME

1. Yu Darvish

2. Didi Gregorius

3. Joey Votto

4. Jose Abreu

5. Carlos Gonzalez

6. Robinson Cano

7. Justin Verlander

8. Yadier Molina

9. Shin-Soo Choo

These players are eager to fly home and visit their families after a long season. Help them find their way by putting the correct number next to the players' homes on the map.

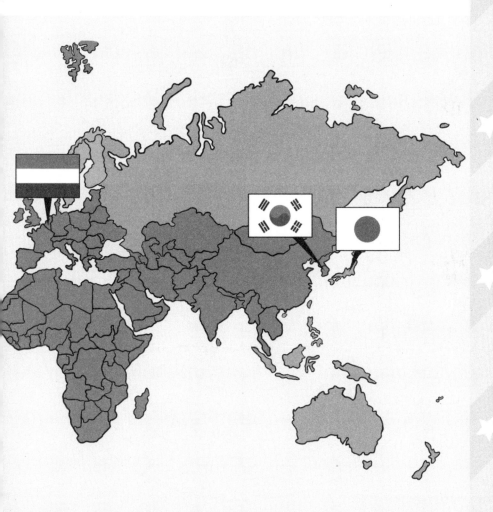

This slugger has been called in to pinch-hit, but he can't find his way to the plate! Help him out by guiding him through this maze.